Gift of the Magpie
A Brotherhood of Shadows Story
By Cathryn Marr

Published by Brokenoggin Books, LLC

PO Box 10

Philo, California, 95466

Visit CathrynMarr.com

Previously, in Soul Keeper…

San Francisco, California

Seven and a half months ago

Forensic enigmalogist Keile Raeburn wheeled the not-quite-lifeless body into the Council of Light's autopsy wing. Sharp on his heels, Council of Light director Celeste Fury followed, dragging a cart full of instruments and a mishmash of blinking and beeping electronic devices. Pediatric psychiatrist Kate Cavanaugh brought up the rear.

"Celeste, this is wrong. Don't do this,"
Kate pleaded. Her voice shook with fear, as

though she'd been pleading with Celeste for a while. "You can't—"

"Who is she?" Ignoring her sometime paramour, Celeste leaned in to attach patches from one of the monitors to the body's temples. "She's older than the others."

"No idea." Keile gave them a questioning side-eye, but only shook his head. "She's at least five or six years older than the others. Mid-to-late teens, maybe, and recently gave birth." He pulled back the sheet that covered the girl. "Aiieeee." He grimaced and made a motion at the victim's torso. "Or rather, a baby was cut out of her at the same time her soul was harvested.

"Oh God," Kate whispered. Fist to her mouth in horror, she shrank against the

stainless-steel coolers where bodies were stored and slid to the floor even as Celeste exclaimed, "What?"

She leaned in to look at the brutal wounds cross-patching the body's belly area. Her expression turned ugly. "Not one of our people, then. And the Nightkeepers wouldn't need to be so—" Her mouth worked. "—careless."

Straightening, she moved to adjust the monitors then attached a lead at the girl's throat, and flipped a couple of dials.

Kate rose to her knees. "Please," she begged. "Don't."

"We'll never learn what they know if we don't," Celeste said harshly. "Aurora Montgomery can't be the only one able to speak with these children."

She punched a button on the monitor and the body's mouth opened. A belch of air issued from it.

"Good." Celeste patted the victim's arm, leaned in close to its ear. "Tell me who took your baby," she whispered. "Help me find him..."

1

Dexter, Michigan

Early December

Tugging her coat tight across her body, Magpie struggled to make headway through the blowing and drifting snow. It was early in the season for Michigan to see blizzard weather. She'd counted on getting here well before winter set in.

She'd been running for the better part of six months, moving from San Francisco to Portland to Seattle, then South and East into Idaho on her way to Wyoming then Montana. Nowhere felt safe. On foot, by bus, and occasionally by train—when she could sneak aboard—she'd traveled almost non-stop, trying to stay away from *him*. *He'd* said he'd be able to find her wherever she was because of his connection to the baby—*his* baby—she'd given birth to almost seven months ago.

At barely sixteen, she didn't even know if she ever wanted children, but in the end, the choice hadn't been up to her. *He'd* chosen her, lured her with promises her hungry mind and body hadn't been able to refuse, then raped her. After that, she'd done what she had to in order to keep herself and her baby safe. She'd run until her options came down to slim and none. That was the point at which she'd finally turned her flight homeward, toward rural Michigan. Four years ago, she'd been so anxious to leave that she'd hitchhiked for twenty-five hundred miles and lived on the San Francisco streets to escape it.

Inside her coat, the baby squirmed inside the soft sling she'd used to strap it to her chest in an effort to keep it safe and warm. It was currently sopping wet, stinky, and hungry, but she was out of diapers and had nowhere to change and feed it in this weather anyway.

"Shh," she whispered to it. "As soon as we're safe for the night."

The infant squirmed harder, taking no reassurance from her words. From the start, it had been a cranky and demanding baby. Teething had not improved its disposition. Neither did trying to keep it fed on formula or milk or the thin gruel-like baby cereal she'd started giving it in an effort to keep it full and quiet. She'd never been particularly fond of babies. This one reminded her why.

To her right, a pinpoint of light twinkled in the gathering dusk. Eagerly, Magpie turned toward the godsend. Out in the middle of nowhere, light often meant shelter. A garage, shed, barn, or out building of some sort—anything to get her and the kid out of this thigh-deep snow and into someplace where she could sit down. Maybe find food and get some sleep, if she was very lucky.

She shifted the fussing baby higher on her chest and tugged at the backpack straps digging into her shoulders. Turning toward the light, she stepped forward. Only snowdrift met her seeking foot. She plunged chest deep into it.

"Damn it, Fish!" she shrieked. He'd been her protector throughout her pregnancy, had gotten her help when she'd needed it most, but he'd also talked her into this current mess. She could *feel* him, as though he was with her, had been watching over her every step of this trying, tiring journey to...here. Tears leaked from her eyes, to make quickly frozen tracks down her cheeks. Where was he now that she needed someone to pull her out of a damn snowbank?

Arms flailing, she tried to turn around to go back the way she'd come. To no avail. Just as she was starting to really panic, headlights swept across her and a vehicle plowed to a stop. The driver's door opened.

"Hey," a feminine voice called. "D'you need help?"

Mouth full of snow, Magpie didn't respond. The baby, however, let out a thin, distressed wail.

"Oh, man, is that a baby?" the voice said. "Hang on! I'm coming."

What seemed an eternity later, a slim woman on snowshoes came up beside her, stooped to dig through the snow, and hooked an arm under Magpie's right shoulder. Magpie struggled to regain her footing without landing on the baby or pulling her rescuer into the drift with her. The baby protested, struggling within its bindings and making the exercise difficult. After a concerted effort, Magpie was upright again.

"Is your baby all right?" the woman asked anxiously.

Shivering, Magpie clutched the squirming lump attached to her chest. The infant made an angry grunting sound and kicked her. "I think so."

Her rescuer laughed. "All right, but not happy, from the sound of it."

Magpie made an unhappy face. "She's never happy."

The woman made sympathetic clucking sounds and pointed toward the headlights illuminating them both. "C'mon. Let's get you into the car." She hiked an arm under Magpie's and took a step toward the road. "Where you headed? I'll take you home."

Magpie panicked. "No, that's all right." The home she'd run away from four years before was another hundred or so miles north. It was where she was headed, sort of, but she wasn't anxious to get there. Arrival would require explanations and recriminations and…

She wasn't ready to face them yet. Especially not with this baby in hand.

She glanced longingly at the pinprick of light that had drawn her into this predicament. All she wanted right now was food and a shelter that was warm enough and safe enough to unwrap the kid and put it down for a while. "If you can just help me back to the road, I'm sure we'll be fine."

"Don't be silly." The woman heaved Magpie out of the ditch and onto the road, drawing her into the glow of the headlights. "Here, let me look at you." Holding Magpie at arm's length, the woman gave her a quick once over. "Why you're just a child!"

Magpie hadn't been a child for nearly as long as she could remember. When she was little more than three, her mother had told her to keep an eye on her baby sisters who were ages two and six months. Leaving the three of them alone in the playroom, her mother gone off to do... Magpie couldn't remember what somewhere else in the house. When a button eye had disappeared from a stuffed animal her baby sister was holding, her mother had blamed Magpie for not keeping a close enough eye on the six-month-old and letting the baby swallow the button. A trip to the hospital and x-rays had ensued. Her baby sister had not swallowed the button, but Magpie had been scolded again and again anyway.

Since then, it seemed there'd always been someone or something to look after, jobs to do that might better have been done by adults, and spankings and scoldings when Magpie hadn't done those jobs right. In order to get away from living in constant fear of doing another thing wrong, Magpie had runaway. Some part of her laughed. The fear and punishment she'd experienced at home was nothing compared to what living on the streets was like. But at least the choices, good and horrendous, had all been hers.

Numb with cold and fatigue, Magpie stared at the dark, featureless woman silhouetted against the headlights. Her voice sounded kind. Magpie wanted to believe that she was, though she hadn't much experience with kindness. Her friend Fish and the people who'd helped her when she was in labor probably qualified, but she hadn't been with them long enough to be sure. Kindness could be deceptive and trust was something she couldn't offer lightly, if ever.

As though sensing Magpie's hesitation, the woman asked gently, "Are you in trouble?" When Magpie stood mute and undecided, the woman hooked elbows with her again. "I'm Bea," she said briskly, guiding Magpie to the vehicle's passenger door and ushering her inside. "I'm just going up to the house there—" She pointed toward the light that had drawn Magpie's attention. "Let's get you and that baby inside and warmed up and we can go from there."

*

A blast of warmth greeted Magpie when Bea ushered her through the door and into the house's mudroom. Closing her eyes, Magpie lifted her face to the heat that leaked into the anteroom from the house's interior. She hadn't felt anything like it in months, maybe years. Warm. Welcoming. *Home.* Tears prickled at the corners of her eyes. She ducked her head so the woman who'd rescued her wouldn't see.

"Get out of those wet things and come inside," Bea urged as she shed her own coat and boots.

Gaze on the light emanating through the window of the door into the home's interior, Magpie tried to unbutton her coat and remove the backpack at the same time. Chuckling, Bea said, "Here let me get this."

In moments, Magpie was free of pack, coat, and boots, and Bea had run a hand along a line of shoes and slippers tucked into cubbyholes beneath a boot bench. She pulled out a pair of fleece-lined slippers and handed them to Magpie.

"We keep spares just in case."

Too exhausted to wonder at her good fortune, Magpie plopped heavily onto the boot bench and accepted the slippers. "Thank you." She had to tuck the bundle of baby close in order to slide into the footgear. The infant protested. Loudly.

Magpie winced and stretched her jaw, trying to block the noise. Leaning back into the wall behind the bench, she hurriedly tried to loosen the baby bundle. Her still icy fingers refused to follow her commands. A tear of frustration leaked from the corner of her eye. She was so...so *bad* at this *mother* thing. If only she hadn't been so stupid about everything. More grown up. Less naïve. Then she wouldn't be stuck in this mess with a baby that wasn't even hers.

Sympathy filled Bea's face as she looked from Magpie to the baby and back. "Come here. Let's get you cleaned up while mama gets out of her wet things, too." She pulled the stretchy sling away from the struggling infant and wiggled her free. Wrinkling her nose and holding the soggy-diapered creature at arm's length, she asked, "What's her name?"

"Dem—" Wincing, Magpie bit her tongue on "Demon Spawn," the only name she'd used for the infant. Instead she said, "Her name is Dehmari," and realized she liked the name. Pleased for thinking of it, she eased out of her coat. "I call her Demi for short."

"Interesting." Bea hoisted the baby and headed into the kitchen. "C'mon, Dehmari. Let's make you dry."

2

Cackleberry Airport, Dexter, Michigan

Early December

Jinx Falken stepped out of the two-seat Cessna 152 and eyed the falling snow with disgust. He'd never been a fan of the white stuff and that opinion hadn't changed in all the millennia he'd been above ground. That's why he lived where the temperatures were warm, or at least moderate, year-round. That was why, sometime around 1867 or so, he'd adopted a drawling accent straight out of America's deep south. Heat suited him. Cold did not. If Luc's intel was wrong, Jinx was freezing his balls for nothing.

Growling, he turned to look for the car that was supposed to be awaiting his arrival. Nothing but empty field and swirling flakes met his gaze. What in almighty hell was he doing here, in *Michigan*, in *December*, chasing a lead that was little more than a suggestion of a hint on the breeze?

A gleeful wind sent a swirl of cold around his ears. He hunched into his shoulders and turned up the fleece collar of his coat. The snow that had collected on it cascaded down the back of his neck in an icy avalanche. Swearing, he brushed at his neck, trying to erase the feeling of frigid cold, knowing he should have picked up a scarf at the same time he'd purchased the puffy jacket he was wearing. He should never have let Solaya's comments convince him to cut his hair at all, let alone to get it sheered not only above his collar, but cropped close to his head as well. He missed having that added insulation to tuck inside his jacket and around his neck right now.

You always were a wuss.

The taunt made Jinx whip around, looking for the person behind the voice, before he realized it was Luceire Garard in his head. Grimacing, Jinx sent back a mental cartoon balloon bubble with the image of a raised middle finger then shut down the telepathic link even as he heard Garard laugh and Rory from the background, *I like your hair*. Damn soul keeper. He knew better than to open himself to anyone who might be listening into the supernatural networks, especially when it came to Luc and Rory. His brother fallen was in hiding to protect his lover while she learned to harness her new abilities. Between them, they were also trying to locate more of the prophesied special children in need of protection from the supernatural beings that wanted to wipe them out before they were born. Older children would also require training in the use of abilities the humans they were born to had no means to understand. That was Rory's task: to teach them what they would need to know in order to survive and thrive. Jinx did not envy this monumental undertaking, especially while they were in hiding.

Which left Jinx in the wilds of Michigan, stamping his feet in the damn snow and cold, waiting for a driver to appear. Because Rory had received a credible, telepathic message suggesting the baby they'd all spent months looking for was here. She could have come after the infant herself by opening a "door" in the world between wherever she and Luc were and here. Except for that pesky "but." As in, but they'd been warned by a woodland fae that if Rory continued to open portals in the world, dangerous factions would be alerted to not only to her whereabouts but to the children she was trying to help.

Luc had steadfastly refused to expose her to any of the remaining council members who'd tried to murder her last spring. After four thousand years of chasing Solaya through history only to have her do something heroic and die every time he got close, Jinx understood Luc's reluctance to mess with a good thing. But damn, Jinx could have sent someone else to check out the story. He hadn't had to volunteer himself. Or let Solaya cut his hair. But he'd wanted the intimacy having her fingers in his hair brought. And he'd needed the escape of this mission when the small intimacy led to her inevitable rejection of the deeper intimacies he'd tried to pursue. Her desire to have him available as long as he remained at arm's length was wearing thin. He'd have to do something about it when—

The sound of something with big tires crunching through the snowpack broke his thoughts. Gratefully he turned as a black Cadillac

Escalade pulled up alongside him. Without waiting for the driver, Jinx opened the closest rear door and climbed into the seat. The driver glanced at Jinx in the rearview mirror.

"You have the address?" Jinx asked as he divested himself of his snowy jacket. The driver gave him an affirmative head tip. "Then let's go."

3

Magpie looked around the sizable kitchen Bea ushered her into. It was a little worn-looking, but inviting.

"There's a bathroom that way." Bea pointed to a hallway off the kitchen. "Get out of those wet things and make yourself comfortable while I wrangle this little creature—" the baby let out an angry, demanding cry on cue, and kicked at Bea who simply turned her, wrapped an arm around her from behind and positioned her on a hip "—and find you something to eat. Do you like eggs?"

Gaze still roving everywhere, taking it all in, Magpie nodded. She'd have said yes to snails right now, but she did love eggs.

"Good." Bea made shooing motions. "Go on now. Get out of those wet things." She laughed at the baby's new wail of protest and headed down the hall she'd pointed Magpie at. "C'mon, infant. Let your mama get cleaned up while I find you something dry. I think one of the girls left disposables here last week..."

Bea's voice trailed off as she headed down the hallway, past the door she'd pointed out to Magpie. Tiredly, Magpie took her backpack with her into the bathroom. Cozy, light sage green walls were offset by fluffy, deep green towels and bath rugs, and softer green accents in complimentary colors. The sink, toilet, and corner bathtub were white. The counter top was a mottled dove-gray marble that matched the walk-in shower's tile. The linen and under-sink cupboards were stained a smokey gray. A seasonal snowman soap dispenser sat next to a Dixie cup dispenser full of Christmas-themed paper cups. Thanksgiving had passed while she was on a bus somewhere, and except to note the intermittent display of Christmas sparklies, she hadn't stopped to think about the solstice holidays. Twinkling white lights framed the small window above the tub. Magpie gazed around in a sort of dazed wonder. She had not experienced anything so clean and luxurious since she'd left home. The thick rug beneath her feet was heaven.

Fearful of dirtying her surroundings, she unzipped her backpack and gingerly placed it on the tiled floor. It sagged open. She made a grab for it before it could spill its contents. It wasn't much, mostly things for the "creature," but it was all she had and she didn't want to lose any of it. She just wished everything was clean.

Speaking of... She reached into the pack and pulled out the last of her clean undies and an overlong, oversized tunic that she kept because it had been stolen and given to her by her friend Fish. She rarely wore it because she didn't like it, but it would do.

With a wistful glance at the bathtub she turned on the shower to warm up the water. It would be bliss to sink into a tub full of hot water and just get warm, but she didn't want to leave Bea alone with the demon child for long. There was no telling what the infant could get up to. It had only started a couple of days ago, but Magpie had witnessed a few things lately that were really not natural—for a baby or anyone else. San Francisco might not look twice at supernatural goings on, but she didn't think the Midwest was ready for a six-month-old levitating itself to get hold of something it wanted that was out of reach—or whisking said object through an intact shop window. Magpie'd had to run and hide more than once because the infant was a thief and she didn't know what to do about it. If it would only steal something useful to their mutual survival...

And their continued mutual survival was exactly the thing. Because this baby wasn't entirely human and Magpie was not equipped to deal with it, especially not long term. Fish had told her to get safe, then start looking for someone who could help both her and the infant. But he hadn't told her where to go or how to find "someone," whoever that might be.

The problem in a nutshell. Finding not only a place that was safe to hide, but also someone to trust with both their lives.

Sighing, she shed her clothing, tested the shower's water temperature, and stepped into the spray.

4

Jinx glared at the snow that had drifted across the back road his driver was trying to take them down. They were stuck, no doubt about it. Why didn't his post-angelic powers extend to hoisting snow out of his path and flinging it to the wind in one fell swoop? Extra strength, speed, and the ability to connect telepathically with members of the Brotherhood were hardly useful when it came to needing to *melt* stuff that was freaking In The Way.

On the other hand, even if he could melt it, there was too much for one go. It would probably flood the entire area, and then he'd feel like an impatient jerk.

He really hated snow.

Disgruntled, Jinx powered down his window and stuck his head out. The driver was silhouetted in the headlights' glow. "What do you think? Can we get through?"

Shaking his head, the driver returned to the door he'd left half-open when he'd dismounted to get an idea of the situation. "Not without help or a snowmobile. I'm sorry I didn't ask for a plow package, sir."

Jinx laughed in spite of himself. "Can't prepare for everything, Joe."

"Unfortunately." Joe climbed back into his seat. "Where now, sir? We should be able to go back the way we came—"

Jinx didn't let him finish. "Is there someplace around here I can rent a snowmobile?"

"Maybe back in town, sir." Joe sounded dubious. "No place will be open tonight."

Jinx swore under his breath. "Fine." It wasn't, if the information he'd received about the

Council of Light being on its way was accurate. He didn't know what Celeste Fury wanted with Magpie and her baby, but the sooner they were found and squirreled away somewhere safe, the better. "Let's go back to town. I'll need a hotel for the night, and a snowmobile in the morning." He could hear the impatience in his voice. This mission was time sensitive, and the blizzard his nemesis. "Can we do that, Joe?"

Joe's head tipped in the affirmative. "I hope so, sir. I'll do my best."

5

Magpie had just finished rinsing the shampoo out of her hair when a shriek she knew all too well sounded from down the hall. She slipped and stumbled, banging her elbow against the shower wall in her hurry to get out, dried, dressed, and down the hall to contain the demon spawn before Bea kicked them back into the storm. The older woman had no idea how apt the "creature" appellation was when it came to Magpie's charge.

Instead of the disaster she anticipated, Magpie found Bea laughing at the baby, who hovered inches above the kitchen sink. Shrieking happily, the infant reached for the Christmas mobile dangling there. When Magpie skidded to a stop in the doorway, Bea made a half-turn and put a finger to her lips.

"She floats," Bea said. Her arms were outstretched in the classic parental "ready to catch it if it falls" gesture.

Magpie shut her eyes and released a sigh. "Do you want us to leave?"

Bea glanced at her in surprise, then back at the airborne creature. "Because Dehmari is the living version of *Jack-Jack*?"

Magpie squinted, trying to place the reference. It took her a minute to connect the name to the youngest member of the animated *The Incredibles* family. But it fit—and was all too apt. *Jack-Jack* was his own version of unpredictable superbaby-demon that no one knew exactly how to handle. The "creature" aka Dehmari aka Demi was all of *Jack-Jack* and more, usually at the worst possible time. When she got the reference, she nodded. "Yes."

Bea pursed her lips, still watching the baby. "Has that happened to you before? You've been kicked out because the little one is special?"

There was no emphasis on the word. No air quotes or verbal italics or judgement. Just the word. Magpie struggled with hope. To want it, but not to have it. "Hope" had been absent from her life for so long.

Deciding it was better to get it over with quickly if things were going to go south, she nodded. "Lots of places. She does other *things*," she said, voice low. "Things..." Bewildered, she raised her gaze to meet Bea's. "Things that aren't *good*. Things I don't understand, that aren't..." She floundered. How to explain a six-month-old's kleptomania. Or the fact that Magpie had seen the infant creature throw a lightning bolt at someone who'd tried to accost them. That Dehmari had instinctively killed that someone in order to protect them both. And she'd given

Magpie such a look of pride afterward that Magpie was fairly certain the baby knew exactly what she'd done and expected to be praised for it. "*Things* I don't know how to explain. Or deal with."

"Hmm," Bea said. "I can see where that might be a problem for some people. Maybe I'll have one, too." She turned and opened the refrigerator door. "Tomorrow you'll tell me your whole story, but not tonight. Right now, you both need food and a safe place out of the storm. If you have formula or something for the baby, I can fix you some eggs. Or we've got today's dinner leftovers. How about some mac 'n cheese and some Christmas cookies?" She glanced over her shoulder at Magpie. "Unless you prefer gingersnaps?"

Some of the fear inside Magpie whooshed out. Her shoulders dropped. It wasn't permanent, but they were out of the cold for tonight. Tomorrow she could figure out something else. She gave Bea a tremulous smile. "I have cereal for her and gingersnaps sound wonderful..."

6

Magpie slept until light filtered through the crack between the insulating blackout curtains in the bedroom at the back of the house. Being comfortable frightened and disoriented her. She jerked upright and looked around wildly, trying to see why the demon spawn was not cuddled tight, kicking her, or otherwise trying to get her attention. A squeal of infant laughter penetrated her panic. She slumped beneath the blankets. Right. Snowstorm. Bea. House. Food. Bed. Comfort. Demon spawn—er, *Dehmari*, Demi for short—being uncustomarily entertaining instead of *"what the bejaysus is that?!"* scary.

Unwilling to leave the quilted warmth, but feeling she should, Magpie dragged herself out of bed, and opened the curtains. More fresh snowfall greeted her, piled high along the side of the house. Across a partially wooded expanse she saw what appeared to be a pseudo parking lot. Snowmobiles in a variety of colors sat in a ragged row. A roughly shoveled passage led to the house. Just where had she ended up last night?

Another baby shriek roused her. Hoping Dehmari wasn't up to some supernatural trick,

Magpie followed the happy screams down the hall.

At least a dozen women were in the kitchen, chattering, drinking coffee, and passing around the baby. Dehmari was clearly in her element. Magpie noted she was not pulling any of her special "tricks", for which she was grateful. She hated being among this many strangers, and if her six-month-old companion had been performing, Magpie doubted these women's reactions would be as accepting as Bea's had been.

Feeling shy and uncomfortable, she looked for her hostess. Bea spotted her first, waved her over, and pressed a plate filled with eggs, sausage, and pancakes with blueberry syrup into her hands. "How did you sleep? I hope you like pancakes."

Overwhelmed, Magpie nodded, whispered "good," and accepted the plate. Eyes wide, she looked at the crowd, back at Bea.

Bea smiled. "We've got holiday orders to fill," she said. At the question on Magpie's face, she laughed. "We make and sell chocolate. Christmas is coming. Lots to do." She pointed her chin at Magpie's plate. "Eat up and I'll show you."

Thirty minutes later, having eaten and reclaimed Dehmari—truthfully, she was really beginning to like the name, and the baby seemed more settled when called by it—she followed Bea through the house and into a walkout basement. Three walls worth of picture windows filled the space with light. An office with an open door

stood open along the fourth wall, and Magpie

could see more windows there. She turned to

look at the main room. And stopped. The shiny

that awaited her gaze did something funny to

Magpie's insides.

Magpie loved shiny things. Had ever since

she was little. It didn't matter what it was—gum

wrappers, keys, lawn ornaments, sequins,

expensive baubles—if it sparkled, she wanted it

and would do whatever it took to acquire it. That

was, in fact, how she'd gotten her name. And this

room—this entire basement, in fact—was chock

full of "shiny". Everywhere she looked, surfaces

shone. She coveted the mysterious, but gleaming

chocolate-making equipment in the "clean

room." She wanted the glossy, fingerprint-less

refrigerator, needed the glimmering pots holding various types of melting chocolate. And the trays! All of it appealed to her in ways she wouldn't have believed possible.

Unaware she was doing it, she stroked a stainless-steel countertop, petted the stainless-steel double sink's glistening faucet. In her arms, the baby leaned way back, studying her. Momentarily distracted, Magpie glanced at her then up at the spoons and ladles hanging overhead. On Magpie's hip, Dehmari did one of her "go faster" wiggles. The fingers on one tiny hand made a "gimme" gesture, and one of the smaller ladles dropped from the rack into it. Dehmari giggled and thwacked Magpie upside the head with it.

"Ow," Magpie said, and relieved the baby of the ladle. Immediately, Dehmari acquired a long spoon in the same fashion. Magpie caught this one before the infant could hit her with it. Dehmari made another grabbing motion at the rack. It started to rattle and bounce, causing the hanging paraphernalia to clang together. A small copper pot hit Magpie in the head before the baby shrieked happily and captured it along with a second spoon.

Behind them, Magpie heard tiny shrieks and squeals from the women coming in from the kitchen. It took her a heartbeat to come back to herself and realize that everyone, not just Bea, had observed what Dehmari was doing.

Holding a hand up between her face and the pot the giggling infant was banging on, Magpie turned to face the shocked women.

"She does stuff, okay?" She could hear the defensiveness in her own voice. Hear a bitterness that surprised her. She'd been too busy keeping them both alive, living hand to mouth, to feel anything, much less something as strong as resentment. She didn't like it. She closed her eyes and breathed. She should never have come here, never have returned to Michigan, never have hoped. "She came this way."

Not "was born this way." "Came this way." Because Dehmari wasn't hers. Fish had taken her baby somewhere to protect it from whoever was looking for it. Dehmari was what she'd been left with, so Michael Beck, the bastard who'd raped not only her but Dehmari's mother—and other impressionable, underage girls as well—in order to impregnate them, couldn't find either baby through his tie to the mothers. But both Fish and Magpie had hoped Dehmari would be "normal."

Whatever "normal" was.

The women watched her uneasily.

"What *is* she?" one of them asked.

A few edged toward the basement door nearest the parking lot and retreat even after Bea said, "Everybody comes with something, right?"

"Sure. But that's not... *right*," someone said.

Eyes wide, others nodded in agreement.

"Can you do that?" Yet another pointed from the now still rack to the pot Dehmari banged on with the spoon she'd levitated off of it.

Feeling cornered, Magpie breathed hard and deep, trying to contain the fear that, once again, she'd be out in the cold with nothing but a kleptomaniac baby. That they would end up freezing to death out there.

Trembling, she shook her head. "No."

She looked at Bea, who firmed her mouth and stepped close, lending warmth and support without touching her. Magpie was glad for the warmth, equally appreciative that Bea didn't touch her. Magpie was pretty sure she'd fall apart completely at a touch.

"Is this something Dehmari's father can do?" Bea asked.

Magpie worked her tongue around her mouth. She looked at everyone with misgiving. She didn't want to think about Dehmari's sire—

her own baby's sire—ever again. "No. I-I... don't know."

When Bea simply stood there, sympathetic, and encouraging, Magpie's resolve firmed. She needed—*they* needed—help from someone, somewhere.

She hesitated for a dozen more heartbeats. Then she blurted out the thing she'd never said aloud before—the thing she'd tried not to even acknowledge. The only true thing she could think of that might distract them from Dehmari's antics and give the two of them any hope of safe haven until the storm passed. "I was raped."

7

It snowed for four days, the white stuff piling up and making even foot travel slow going.

Acquiring any kind of transport was an exercise in futility. He couldn't even find cross country skis to rent. Getting hold of snowshoes was impossible. Everything was shut down. Not even snowplows were out in it.

Stuck in his hotel room with nothing to do except stare at the snow gave Jinx plenty of time to work out why neither snowshoes nor skis would be of any use if he wanted to bring Magpie and the baby back with him. He'd reached the point where he also didn't believe a snowmobile would be useful. It was cold out there and the baby was too small and delicate to be out in the frigid wind and icy "real feel" temperatures for so long. Hell, *he* was too small and delicate to be out there.

And his hair was still too damn short for this weather.

Forced inactivity made him grumpy. Doing nothing made him restless, which made him question his life's purpose. He hated it. He'd dived out of heaven and crawled over crushed glass and molten lava to get out of the pit because The Divine had once told him there would come a point in his existence when he would have to "go see about a girl"—which he'd been doing for over four thousand years. Same girl, same song, and very little variation in the dance. She died every time and he had to wait until she reincarnated to do it all over again. He was stuck in a damn time loop, a version of the movie *Groundhog Day*, and the whole thing had gotten very, *very* old.

He prowled his hotel room, feeling growly and kneecapped. He was a big bad fallen angel with a dozen supernatural gifts, not one of which was practical here and now.

By the fifth morning, he couldn't stand it any longer. Being and feeling helpless didn't suit him—hell, he'd leaped out of heaven and crawled out of the pits of hades because he'd felt helpless to change anything where he was. He was a doer, not a thinker—a thug, not the brains behind the thuggery.

Except that's exactly what he'd had to become as leader of the Brotherhood of Shadows. The brains, the planner, the head.

Disconcerted by the thought, Jinx headed outside at the first sound of a snowplow in the hotel parking lot. He had to get out of here, away from his treacherous thoughts. He needed action. Smashing things. Punching bad guys. Rescuing babies. Something he could accomplish without thinking about it.

The air was sharp, filled with stinging, cutting snow particles. The storm had left everything white and pristine. Snow drifted high up the sides of buildings, and a good eighteen-to-thirty inches deep wherever it was flat.

Wind had made whorls across the undisturbed snow's surface, trees hung heavy with lumps of white, and birds and light-footed wildlife had left behind tracks for the initiated to read. Even the air seemed to sparkle in the sunshine's glare. Jinx appreciated the beauty for half a tick before a gust of wind threw snow into his face. Glowering, he ducked deeper into his hood and swiped the cold spray off his face and goggles. Barely nine a.m. and already this was not shaping up to be one of his favorite days.

He looked around, wondering if he'd be able to get out of here today. He was tall, but the mounds made by the plows were high, well over head height on him. Since he'd come into being when the divine created the principalities, he'd never seen so much snow in one place. Had deliberately managed to avoid it, truth be told. He hoped to never see it all in one place again.

The sound of a 4x4 pickup truck crunching across snow pack caught his attention. The vehicle pulled up beside him. Joe's face appeared in the open driver's side window.

"Got a line on snow capable transport for you."

Jinx lifted an eyebrow in question.

A grin lurked around Joe's pursed his lips. "You'll need to buy it though, couldn't find a rental on short notice."

Jinx narrowed his eyes. "Why don't I like the sound of that?"

"Depends on how you feel about spending fifty grand on a used vehicle that you want to use once." When Jinx grimaced, Joe laughed. "Trust me. Get in. This thing is one of a kind. You'll like it."

The best part of the day later, Jinx was the dubious new owner of what amounted to a monster truck slash camper van on tracks. Hating the delay, the snow, the vehicle's slow but deliberate pace through the snow, and the fact that it was nearly full dark by four o'clock, he returned to his hotel room for one last night of no sleep.

The following pre-dawn, when the sky was starting to go soft around the edges, he was back at the country crossroad he'd found himself at with Joe almost a week ago. Magpie's energy signal had faded to almost nothing. Damn it. Picking up energy *pings* was so not his forte. He should have swallowed his pride and asked Solaya for a locator spell specific to Magpie. But she'd have wanted to bargain and...

He couldn't do it. He'd loved that damned sorceress for over four thousand years, and he still couldn't figure her out.

Feeling out of his depth, Jinx sent Luc and Rory a quick telepathic comic book bubble, *"Where next?"*, but got no answer. Either they'd gone deep underground or were somehow out of range or Luc wasn't picking up because it was too dangerous.

Antsy and on his own, Jinx scanned the too-white countryside. It was almost as though someone had managed to mask his quarry somehow, surrounding them with an obfuscation spell the way Luc had informed him had happened with the child he and Rory had found in Oregon at Halloween. But it didn't really feel like a spell. Or not exactly. More like...

Magpie wasn't sending as hard as she had been because she didn't feel threatened. Was more relaxed and less afraid.

The thought stopped him cold. Wherever she and the baby were, maybe she did feel safe—at least temporarily. Powerful emotions were easier to pick up on, as his time with Solaya had taught him. Fear was one of the most powerful, the most easily detected by predators like him.

The thought of himself as a predator was no longer even a faint *blip* on his conscience. He *was* an apex predator. Well controlled, but still. Leaping out of heaven and into the pit he'd climbed out of had made him what he was the same way it had made the angels who'd chosen to follow Mephisto what they were. He'd accepted what he was long, long ago. Not liking what he was wouldn't change it. Acceptance and control kept him sane.

Now if only he could get Solaya to understand that. Her inability to accept him as he was stung, but he'd managed to reach her, gain her acceptance and love two hundred and ninety-seven times before. It was harder this time around than it had ever been, but he was nothing if not patient. He could wait out her reluctance, her wholesale distrust of him and his kind. And hopefully, when all was said and done, she would choose him again…

Yanking himself out of his druthers, he regarded the snowy terrain. *Stay on mission*, he told himself. *Find the baby, save the girl. Worry about Solaya later.*

Grimacing, he turned back to the Snowcat. If he stuck within a five-mile radius of Magpie's last strong ping, it was still a lot of area to cover. And if Magpie felt safe, *was* safe for the moment, he needed to be a little smarter than usual in order to find her.

Checking the GPS coordinates for the spot where Magpie's energies had last pinged, Jinx climbed back into the Snowcat, put it in gear, and crunched cross country over the piled-high snow toward his target.

<h1 style="text-align:center">8</h1>

Dexter, Michigan

Mid-ish December

Telling the women who worked with Bea that she'd been raped had gone better than Magpie hoped.

For more than a year, she'd avoided thinking about how both Dehmari and her own missing baby came to be. Avoided thinking about how Dr. Michael Beck had started to play on her emotions during a session.

A child psychologist, he'd allegedly come into the homeless camps to help teen runaways find their way. Instead, he'd singled out girls as young as eleven who'd been through their first menses, stroking their egos and praising them one moment, tearing them down the next. And all the while he'd touched them, plying them with sedatives and alcohol to help them "relax" for their private "sessions."

She drew a shaky breath. She didn't want to think about him, what he'd said, how he'd destroyed her both physically and emotionally. Siphoned the trust out of her.

Instead, she thought about how the women who worked with Bea had treated her. They'd been horrified then solicitous, and not one of them suggested she'd brought the rape on herself. That was what she'd feared most—that they'd blame her for what had happened to her. For becoming a victim. For allowing it to happen.

But they hadn't. They'd treated her with empathy, because she wasn't the only rape victim among them, and with sympathy. And though their suspicions about the baby weren't allayed, they were nevertheless trying to accept not only Magpie but also the more *unique* qualities of the now nearly seven-month-old Dehmari.

Almost a week and a half had passed, since Bea had found her and Dehmari in the snowdrift. While Magpie was worlds more comfortable in the chocolate maker's company, she was still self-conscious any time she found the other women's gazes on her. It was hard not to wonder what they thought of her underneath the wary camaraderie—especially since Dehmari was once again teething and given to sudden unhappy bursts of temper. That was when anything that wasn't nailed down was likely to be physically swept up inside her tornado-like misery and flung willy-nilly at anyone who wasn't paying attention.

Magpie had spent every one of the last however many days wondering how long this respite from running could last. Wondering why Bea and the others continued to put up with her and Dehmari now that the snow had finally stopped falling. It would be too easy to get used to this, to take this apparent safety for granted. She couldn't afford to do that. Couldn't afford to believe that this might last for even another hour, let alone days.

She looked around. Maybe it was all the shiny equipment or the fascinating ritual of making the chocolate that made her not want to leave here. Or maybe it was the plethora of Christmas decorations and the season itself that gave her hope.

Or maybe it was just Dehmari's delighted giggles when one of the ladies tickled her, or handed her a spoon to play with, or set her on the floor in front of a stack of pots and urged her to bang on them. Or when she screamed with delight over the Christmas train that tootled around its tracks on the coffee table in the living room slash breakroom.

Whatever it was, Magpie knew that, at least for the moment, she was content. Maybe even happy. She liked helping with the chocolate making, liked shining up the equipment every night. She didn't know how long it had been since she'd felt even a little bit of this.

Bea touched her arm. "We have—" she began and stopped at the sound of a knock on the door upstairs. She turned to one of the women. "We didn't have a tour scheduled for today, did we?"

The other woman shook her head. "Not in this weather." She stepped over near one of the windows that would give her a view of the door as well as the snowmobiles everyone used to get to and from work. "Man. Driving a Snowcat." A second later she stepped sideways and turned to Bea. "He's big." She sounded concerned. "Very big."

Bea looked at Magpie. "Someone you know?"

Frightened, Magpie ducked her head and shrank into herself. "I don't think…" There had been guys at the place where she'd given birth to her own missing baby, but she'd been in labor and didn't really remember them. They hadn't stayed long in any case. She did have a vague memory of the women who'd been in the room with her while she gave birth, but… Fearful, she shook her head. "No."

Bea gave her an assessing glance, then jutted her chin at Dehmari, gestured toward a back room where they packed boxes to be sent out. "Why don't you start packing the cartons for the senior center Christmas party. Close the door."

"But what if... I can't let you—"

"Go." Bea gave her a light push toward Dehmari. "Get the baby and try to keep her quiet." She glanced around at the women. "We'll handle things out here."

Feeling guilty, for what she didn't know, Magpie looked back and forth between the baby, the packing room door, and the women, torn between the desire to trust them to protect her, and the need to do the right thing. To not endanger them by her presence.

The knock at the door turned into pounding. Uncertainty gave way to decision. Magpie grabbed Dehmari, the spoon the baby had been playing with, and a teething cookie that she'd brought down from the kitchen. She carried everything into the packing room and shut the door. Praying that none of the ladies would be harmed on her behalf.

9

Pissed and grumpy over leaving the pristine snowfall covered in rolling tracks while getting precisely nowhere in his search for Magpie, Jinx called Solaya. Or rather, he tried to call Solaya. His cell phone reception left something to be desired despite the now clear blue sky and sparkling landscape.

When he finally got through, she was snappy and sounded...

Uncharacteristically worried about him.

The thought surprised him, since they had not been on the best of terms during her current lifetime—except when it came to sex. In that one area, they were more compatible than ever. Sex with Solaya was always wild and untamed, hungry.

But.

Always, at least in this lifetime, there was a "but." But she didn't want him to kiss her and refused to kiss him. But no biting, no feeding, no vampiring in any way, shape or form. But they could be fuck buddies but not friends.

This had been ongoing since the start of their relationship in this incarnation six years ago. She'd been twenty-two then, and he'd been tired of waiting for her to come to him. He'd agreed to every stipulation she put on their relationship, hoping that eventually she'd remember him, or at least come to see him as more than a blood sucking parasite.

He hadn't been a blood sucking parasite in at least six thousand years, long before their first lifetime together. He required blood as sustenance, yes. But he'd been making do with light repasts from volunteer donors, or pig and bovine blood for millennia. In the last century, he'd been able to use blood bank donations that were at their use-by. And seven months ago, he'd even tried to stop drinking blood entirely, but that...

Had gone badly to the point where Luc had to literally hold him down while Solaya's twin brother Senn squeezed several pints of donated blood into him.

"Jinx, did you call for a reason?" Solaya asked now, bringing him back to the conversation. Or lack thereof. Whenever it came to talking about even the most mundane things, the silence between them was immense.

Jinx blew a puff of air into the cold. His breath hung suspended before him for a moment before dissipating. "I hate to ask," he said, "but I need a locator spell. You're the only sorceress I know who might be able to provide one."

"What happened to the tag Kessie put on her and the baby?"

"Dead or non-existent," Jinx said. "I had Magpie's for a while, but it's faded. Never did pick up the baby's."

He heard Solaya suck air through her teeth. A sound of worry he recognized.

"I don't like that," she said. Jinx heard another huff of air, this time thoughtful. "Give me a few minutes. I'll see what I can do."

Then she hung up.

Twenty-five frigid minutes later she called back. "Do you have a focus?"

Straight to the point, no niceties. Jinx eyed his dubious-looking camper van cum homemade Snowcat. It was larger by several thousand times than most focuses, but, hey, it was what it was.

"Yes."

"Good. Cup your hand around it and concentrate."

Jinx pulled off one puffy snowmobile mitten and placed his bare hand over the engine where it was warmer. "Ready."

Silence answered him as Solaya inaudibly did her thing at the other end of the connection. As completely as possible, Jinx fixed his whole attention on the vehicle. Heat flared between him and it, arced out to encompass the area around him. All at once a ray of violet light shot straight across the field he was standing in, curving slowly but inexorably toward the southwest. If he could tesseract like Rory...

"Do you have it?" Solaya's voice sounded strained and breathless.

"Got it. Thank you."

"Just find those kids and bring them home."

She hung up.

Keeping a hand on his vehicle at all times, Jinx slid around to the door, climbed in, and followed the beam of light.

Trembling, Magpie huddled in the packing room with Dehmari. The baby reached up and patted her face, demanding attention. Magpie looked at her. Dehmari pointed at the room's door and let out what sounded exactly like the Hollywood version of a demonic growl. Magpie started and nearly dropped her. Of all the things the infant had done since their arrival at Bea's, this frightened her more than teleported or floating toys, more than the teething tantrums that often resulted in Magpie ending up bruised when the floating toys were thrown at her. When Dehmari deliberately pointed at the door, growled again, and made giddyap motions on Magpie's hip, Magpie shook her head.

"We can't," she whispered. "Danger. We're keeping safe."

In response, Dehmari squealed and again made an imperious gesture at the door before giving Magpie's cheek a hard *thump* with her head.

"*Ow!*" Magpie gave the infant a light smack on the leg. "No. Stop. Dang—" she broke off the word at the sound of raised voices elsewhere in the house.

"*I know she's here,*" a man said. "*I followed her.*"

The voice was cultured though angry. Magpie didn't recognize it, but was sure it wasn't Michael Beck. His voice had been more... tenor. Almost singsong. As though he'd been used to addressing and luring small children. A children's show host.

In her arms, Dehmari growled louder and jerked at Magpie's shirt, trying to urge her toward the door.

"I don't know what to tell you." Bea's voice. *"I didn't have to let you in, but I do and you tell me I'm lying. There are no little girls here."*

"You followed a sixteen-year-old girl?" One of the other women. *"Isn't that like stalking?"*

Something that sounded like a fist smashing into a wall rattled the house. Immediately, Dehmari snarled and *reached* for the door behind which they hid.

"No—" Magpie said, and clutched the infant tighter.

Too late. The door splintered and exploded outward. Snarling and growling like a demented demon, Dehmari flung them both out of the room, through the gathered women, and into the face of a man who was not Michael Beck. No, this was someone badder than bad. Someone Magpie remembered seeing only once in Beck's company.

A man who was not a man because Magpie had seen him go full on demon.

Savitri Nousaine.

11

Jinx followed the light to where it ended at a sizable dark red house set back among the trees. He'd pulled into the drive and was making his way to where he could see a long, barnlike structure behind it when someone came flying out of the building as though expelled by a canon. A shower of wood and glass rained down to litter the snow, someone else's snowcat, and the collection of snowmobiles parked behind the house.

"What the...?"

Swearing, Jinx slammed on his camper-cat's heavy brakes. He had the vehicle in park and was out of it almost before it juddered to a halt. He crossed the heavy snow at a run, sinking halfway to his knees at every step. His initial thought was that Aurora Montgomery had somehow gotten here and was blowing things up because a) there was a problem, and b) she could.

When he reached the ejected person, he found Savitri Nousaine, fallen angel, former vampire, and former self-proclaimed Master of the West Coast. Former because the aforementioned Aurora Montgomery had stripped him of his demonic half and turned him wholly human last spring. Jinx had thought Nousaine incarcerated by the Council of Light or the Nightkeepers, but apparently not. Or at least not any longer.

He worked his mouth around the thought and looked down at Nousaine who blinked at him and tried to lift a hand to brush the debris out of his face. Neither the hand nor the arm it was attached to appeared to work properly. Jinx looked from Nousaine to the house, where a dozen or so shocked women looked at him through the hole created by the explosion. How in the name of all that was holy had Nousaine—

in his now human form—beaten the Brotherhood to the end point of Magpie's signal?

"Anyone hurt?" he called.

"Only him," someone yelled back.

Nodding, Jinx squatted beside Nousaine to run a hand over the other man's useless arm. "Broken." He pointed at Nousaine's face. "Cuts, abrasions, contusions. Possible broken jaw." Felt along Nousaine's torso, down each leg, and his other arm while Nousaine grimaced in human pain. "Probable broken bones in both legs and your other arm." Jinx snorted. "You're a mess. What, did you forget you're human now? That the Soul Keeper took your teeth?"

Nousaine attempted to snarl at him through a rapidly swelling jaw.

Jinx winked at him. "Hold that thought."

Righting himself, he risked contacting Luc to warn him that someone from their own forces or possibly the Council's was working with Nousaine. Luc responded by suggesting Jinx have the Brotherhood's mole in the Nightkeepers look into a possible leak.

Though neither of them acknowledged the thought, each knew the other suspected Council of Light leader Celeste Fury of working with forces the Brotherhood opposed to eradicate the special children Jinx's people had sworn to protect.

That settled, Jinx put out a telepathic call for the nearest member of the Brotherhood of Shadows to come deal with Nousaine and his injuries. When response came back that someone would be able to reach them by snowmobile within twenty minutes, he returned to his camper-cat and retrieved a space blanket to cover Nousaine. The ex-fallen was looking shocky, and dazed, suffering from pain in a way he hadn't ever had to in his entire existence. Jinx figured it had to be quite the wake-up call to suddenly find oneself going through what humans went through every day.

After making the former demon-slash-psi-vamp as comfortable and warm as possible, Jinx left him lying in the snow as he turned and headed for the hole in the house.

Inside was chaos. Ceiling tiles and plaster dripped into the room. Splintered wood sagged around the door, but there was less overall damage to the place than Jinx had first assumed.

"I'm looking for a girl and her baby," he told them. "I think there will be more like him—" He jerked his head toward where Nousaine lay. "—after her."

As one, the women shrank from him, closing ranks around someone or something at their center. One of them hefted a heavy-looking pot.

Disregarding their protective stance, he stepped closer and attempted to peer over them and into the middle of their huddle. Height gave him an advantage. He caught a glimpse of the left half of a girl's frightened, but fiercely determined face, honey-colored hair, and a slim body curled protectively over something. That *something* appeared to be gibbering ferociously and trying to lift her off of itself.

Sadness mixed with anger filled Jinx. He'd found Solaya dead, in much the same pose, trying to shield their daughter during the eruption of Vesuvius that had wiped out Pompeii. He refused to remember the countless times after that when he'd found the woman his soul was bound to, dead in an effort to protect and defend the helpless, the defenseless, the powerless…

"My name is Jinx Falken. I was there when your baby was delivered," he said gently. "My—" He almost said "girlfriend", but not only would Solaya have killed him if she heard, "girlfriend" was hardly the right term to describe her and their relationship in any incarnation. "My friends Solaya and Kessie helped you. Your friend Fish was there. You disappeared before we could get you safely away somewhere."

As though by magic, he heard the squabbling whatever that the girl was hiding go quiet. The girl raised her head to peek at him through the curtain of hair that fell across her face.

"I don't know you."

"No." Jinx smiled. "You were a little preoccupied when Luc and Rory brought you to my place to deliver your baby. Fish called you Magpie because you like shiny things."

12

Magpie sat up and scooted around so she could get a better look at the man who peered down at her. She had a vague memory of a tall, blond man with a runner's build who'd greeted them at the security door of his club when the really big guy—Luc, she thought was his name—carried her in and up to the room where she'd endured the worst pain of her life in giving birth.

Inside the cocoon of her arms, Dehmari squirmed until she could poke her head up to look over Magpie's shoulder. The moment she caught sight of the man, she squealed and started to bounce, holding her arms up and reaching for him.

The man who said his name was Jinx, laughed. "I'm glad to see you, too." He put out his hands to the infant.

Unsure what to do, Magpie clutched Dehmari to her chest. Unhappy at not being released *at once* into Jinx's arms, the baby shrieked with rage. Then she leaned in and bit Magpie's ear.

"*Ow!*" She loosened her hold on Dehmari, who immediately tried to crawl into Jinx's outstretched hands. Defeated, Magpie handed her over. "Fine," she said, "but if he murders you, I told you so."

Laughing, Jinx lifted Dehmari, tossed her ceilingward, and caught her. He positioned her in the crook of his elbow and tickled her. "Hello, miss."

Delighted, Dehmari patted his cheeks between her hands and bounced in his arms.

Jinx looked from Dehmari to Magpie and back. Gestured at the hole in the door where snow had started to blow in.

"Did you do this?" he asked the baby.

In response, Dehmari bounced in his arms, head bobbing. She made motions with her hands and arms, all the while jabbering for all she was worth.

Jinx grimaced. "I'll take that as a yes." He turned to Magpie. "Is there somewhere we can talk?" He glanced at the shocked women. "Privately?"

She gave him an uncertain shrug. "I guess?"

She started to gesture toward the stairs to the main part of the house. Bea stepped between her and Jinx.

"You don't have to do this," she told Magpie. She reached for Dehmari who was too enamored with the tassels on Jinx's hood to leave him. She shrugged away from Bea's grab, cuddling in to Jinx, who grinned. He rubbed Dehmari's back.

"You're a handful, aren't you?"

Dehmari tipped her head back to look up at him, telling him something important but unintelligible.

"Uh huh. I see." He turned to Bea and tipped his head toward the blown-out door where the snow had started to drift in. "If you've tarps or something, I'll get this closed over for you until you can get someone out to fix it. I'll cover the costs."

Magpie shrank even further into herself. "I'm so sorry," she whispered. "I didn't know she could—"

"How could you know?" Bea patted her arm and grimaced, looked at Jinx. "Who are you exactly? Magpie seems to know you, but I don't. You don't get to walk in here and—"

"I'm the guy who can help her with this kid."

"I see." Bea studied him for a long moment. When he didn't look away, her mouth tightened. "I have insurance to take care of the house—"

"What are you going to tell your broker? That a baby blew up your house in some kind of act of God to protect you from an ex-demon?" Jinx shook his head. "I don't think that'll fly."

Bea huffed out an impatient breath. "No, but a gas leak might."

"Because it works as a throwaway line in all the paranormal shows?" He grinned when Magpie came out of herself far enough to give him side-eye. "What?" he asked. "I watch television."

She managed a half-hearted snort. "When?"

"When I'm not chasing down missing kids who think they have to handle this—" He jiggled Dehmari, who laughed. "—and what goes along with it alone."

"I had to." She looked all the way up at him. "I didn't want to... Somebody had to—*has* to..." She stopped and glanced uneasily sideways at Bea and the other women.

"I know. But it shouldn't have to be you." Jinx gestured toward the stairs she'd started to lead him toward. "Let's talk."

13

Magpie led the way upstairs. Jinx carried Dehmari, who seemed to have adopted him as a giant plaything. Bea followed, close on Jinx's heels.

Magpie could feel her rescuer's anxiety, an itch between her shoulder blades. The urge to wriggle her shoulders, reach around and scratch, grew more urgent with every step. She didn't know what Jinx Falken wanted to talk with her about, but the idea of listening to what he had to say scared her. Because whatever he said, and no matter how she felt about it, it would mean a change of some sort.

When she'd lived at home, she'd been angry and defiant, unable to remember a time when she hadn't hated someone or something. Since running away from home four years ago, she'd spent almost every minute of every day uncertain, angry, defiant, and very, very afraid. By now, she was used to fear. She didn't like being afraid, but the idea of swapping constant apprehension for something more stable, maybe even better, scared the daylights out of her.

The possibility that he wasn't here to put her on a path to something better terrified her even more.

When they reached the kitchen, she gathered her courage and turned to confront him. "What do you want?"

Yeah, belligerent defiance was always her go-to backup plan when things went sideways. Which they had, big time. It was rarely useful, but attitude was sometimes all she had.

Jinx sat at the kitchen table in a chair that looked too small for him. "To help. And her." He plunked Dehmari on the tabletop, emptied the napkin holder, and handed it to her to play with, then sandwiched her inside the loose ring of his arms. Sheltering her while she played.

Magpie gazed longingly at that protective circle. Wishing she could go back to a time when someone could do the same for her. *Would* do the same for her.

"Why are you here?" she asked.

Jinx cast a significant glance at the kitchen window, through which they could see two people loading Savitri Nousaine onto an evacuation sled attached to a snowmobile. "Same answer," he said. "To make sure you're safe from the likes of him."

Watching Dehmari bang the table with the napkin holder, Magpie folded her lips over her teeth before she nodded. "But—"

Jinx shook his head, looked from Magpie to Bea. "Do you want to keep this private?"

"I…" Hesitant, Magpie chewed the inside of her cheek. "I don't know. Maybe?"

"I don't know who he is, but don't let him intimidate you. You don't have to talk with him alone." Bea said.

Magpie blinked back unexpected tears. She couldn't remember the last time someone normal had stood up for her. Fish wasn't what anyone would call normal, and everyone else she'd had contact with in San Francisco… Well, none of them had been human, so definitely not normal.

"I..." She swallowed around the lump in her throat. Bea had been nothing but kind to her. If she stayed to support Magpie through whatever Jinx Falken had to say, Bea might learn things about her that would change all that. She looked at the Christmas angels stenciled in the kitchen window panes. "I don't..."

Bea sighed and nodded. "We all have things we'd rather other people not know about us, especially when we don't know them well and want them to like us."

"It's not..." Magpie started.

Bea's mouth formed a sad moue. "I know," she said gently. "You trust me, but only so far. I understand."

She rose to leave. Magpie grabbed her hand in mute plea. She wanted to trust Bea all the way. She needed someone with her when she faced whatever was to come next.

Even if it meant Bea rejected her afterward.

"Please…"

Bea looked at her, turned to Jinx, who turned his palms up in a clear *it's up to you*. She sat down and took Magpie's hand in both of hers. "I'm here."

14

Jinx looked around the kitchen and what he could see of the house. Other than to make sure *Carpe Noctem* was decorated, he didn't really celebrate the season himself. Still, he recognized the real thing when he saw it. Christmas—the scent, shape, and colors of it—
was everywhere. Fake snow stencils of angels

and fir trees decorated the windows. Brightly colored toy ornaments were piled in a box near the sink, presumably where the baby could reach them. Cedar garlands with lights wrapped into them were strung around doorways. But more than that, the entire place *felt* like Christmas, felt like acceptance, like home.

Like love.

Tipping his head, he studied Bea as she canted herself forward in her seat, reflexively angling her body as though to put herself between him and Magpie. Keeping an eye on him, she also reached out one hand toward the baby—who laughed at her and scooted her butt closer to him. When Bea gave her a look, the infant laughed harder, clapped her hands, then looked at the Christmas toy box. A variety of crocheted stuffed toys rose on cue and appeared to fling themselves at Bea. It was clearly a game they'd played before, since Bea only snorted and wagged a finger at the tiny miscreant. The toys dropped to the floor.

Watching them, he almost felt bad about what he'd come here to do. A glance toward the blast zone the baby had caused—with good reason, but still—reminded him of why he had to do it.

He took very little seriously. Gravity was a lot of work he didn't have time for. He could however, be circumspect. Normally, Solaya was the only person who brought out verbal caution in him. But looking at Magpie, holding tight to her rescuer in the hope that he wasn't going to disturb her entire world, made him take a step backward and consider what he'd had to say. And how to say it.

He turned his attention from Magpie to Bea and back. "I don't know how much you've told her about what happened to you in San Francisco," he told Magpie and switched his attention to Bea, "or how much she wants you to know."

Within the circle of his arms, Dehmari banged the napkin holder on the table, then made it float. Jinx smiled and grimaced. He knew how expressive his face could be and normally tried to keep his emotions to himself. This baby made that impossible. His lips twisted as sadness filtered through him when he looked at Magpie.

"You can't keep her, you know," he said baldly.

He watched as Magpie clenched Bea's hand tightly and looked away. When Bea started to protest, he raised a hand. "Let me finish."

She subsided, but not willingly. Adjusted her posture to reclaim her hand from Magpie in order to slide her arm around the teen's shoulders. Protective and comforting at once. Jinx watched them for a moment, decided treading carefully would just delay the inevitable.

"I know you ran to protect yourself and your baby from Michael Beck," he said at last. "But he's dead and can no longer hurt or hunt you. I'm not sure yet—" heavy emphasis on the "yet" because when he returned to San Francisco, he would find and destroy whoever *was* hunting and terrorizing children "—how the guy out there—" he flapped a hand toward the parking area behind the house "—found you, but you're no longer linked to Michael Beck in any way."

By the quick intake of breath, the tensing of her shoulders, and the half-frightened, half-hopeful glance she cast toward Bea, Magpie hadn't known. He nodded. The next part would be the hard one for her.

"The thing is..." He paused, looking for any sign from her that he should stop, or that she wanted Bea to leave before he continued. When there was none, he said, "The thing is," he repeated, gentling his tone, "I know this isn't your child. Do you know where your son is?"

The moment Bea gasped and loosened her grip on her hand, Magpie felt the gut punch as though it were a physical thing. She pulled away and hunched into herself, afraid to look at her savior.

"You kidnapped Dehmari? Stole her from her mother?"

"I–I..." Magpie sent Jinx a pleading look. "No. I–she... Her mother..."

"Dehmari's mother was killed," Jinx said, tightening his arms and hunching more protectively around the baby. "I believe Magpie was convinced that the only way to keep both babies safe was to trade them so people like him—" again he pointed toward the parking lot "—wouldn't be able to find either infant."

"But…" Nonplussed, Bea sat back, gaze going from Magpie to Jinx and back. "I don't understand."

Jinx slid his hands into Dehmari's armpits and hoisted her so she could stand. When she dropped the napkin holder, she immediately *reached* for it. It floated into her hands. "You've seen what she can do—"

"She's special," Magpie interrupted quietly. She held out her hands to the baby, who bounced happily and sailed the holder into them. "Her mother was raped by the same man who raped me. There was a bunch of us that happened to. We all got pregnant. We were told the babies—that we—would be traceable through their link to the man who sired them.

"A friend of mine arranged for us to swap babies after they were born. None of us knew who would have anyone else's baby, and none of us would know where the others were. And we hoped no one would be able to trace either the babies or us."

She looked down at her hands. "It doesn't look like we were successful."

"It took six-and-a-half months to find you," Jinx pointed out. "We're still looking for a lot of you."

Anger fluttered through Magpie. "Not for *us*," she said bitterly, "just the babies. The special ones. The ones that c'n do things you can't."

Jinx sipped air, blew it out. Anger shimmered just beneath the surface of his gaze. "No," he said flatly. "Not just the babies. You,

Magpie. You and every girl like you who's been coerced or raped. Every teen, every person who's been duped, bullied, and abused by people like Michael Beck who think they're above the laws of heaven and earth. Every child who sacrificed a home and safety to take care of the infants gotten on them by a sociopath with a god complex and an agenda."

He paused and his gaze on her grew more intense, but his anger softened. "You, Magpie. You."

16

Jinx watched the teen try to work her mind around what he'd said. Watched Bea try to take it in, too. Though unsure about trusting his word, he could see they both wanted to believe him. Even though Bea didn't look like she understood what, exactly, she might be trying to believe.

Between his hands, the baby bounced, *reaching* for everything not within range. Jinx was willing to bet the name "Dehmari" was a quick bastardization of the phrase "demon child." He swallowed a bittersweet smile. Given her origins and burgeoning aptitudes, the name fit her to a T.

"There are a couple of ways we can do this." He focused his attention on Magpie, with a sideways glance at Bea.

"I...I don't want you to take her," Magpie said softly. Once again, Bea leaned toward her, offering support, however uncertainly.

Jinx heard the "but" she didn't say.

"Yes." He nodded. "But. But she's already doing things no one anticipated and she'll only get stronger as she gets older."

"That," Magpie said. Her voice was nearly inaudible. "But—"

"*No.*" Jinx reached out to seize a very shiny knife out of the air before Dehmari could grab it. Her face clouded over. A thwarted wail issued from her. "No," he repeated firmly, showing her the paring knife. "Tool. *Not* a toy."

A second knife flew out of the knife rack, sharp, pointy tip aimed directly at him.

Bea, gasped, paled, and tried to move to intercept the weapon.

Magpie squeaked, "Dehmari, *no...*"

"*No!*" Jinx stuck out a hand and snatched the filet knife from the air.

Dehmari's face grew red. She opened her mouth wide and *screamed*. Glass shattered, crockery burst, the entire house rattled. Jinx picked her up, turned her around, and cuddled her tightly against his shoulder, rubbing her back in soothing circles. "Shhh, Demi, shh," he murmured. "There, there, little one. I know. I know. You want to stay with Magpie, but this is the reason you can't. You might hurt her. Then how would you feel?"

The baby pushed away from his shoulder, and looked at him. When he continued to rub her back, she screamed once in frustration and banged her forehead into his nose as hard as she could. Then she collapsed against him, sobbing the way only babies can sob. The earthquake-like rumble and rattle that shook the house and its contents subsided. Within moments, her sobs tapered off into ragged huffs of heartbroken breath. Her eyelashes met her cheeks, and she slept.

Bea breathed. "How...what...I can't...*this* can't..."

Tears streaked Magpie's face. "I... I..." Lost, she crossed her arms on the table and sank face down into them.

Jinx reached across the table and cupped her arm in his free hand, stroking his thumb over it. "Time to stop runnin', Babygirl." His voice broadened, took on the soft drawl of the deep South he'd cultivated sometime around the Civil War. "You've done everythin' anyone could ask of you. More. But it's time to let go, let someone older and more experienced take the reins."

Magpie's breath hitched in a sob, but she raised her head to see him. "It's just so hard."

"I know." He stroked her arm. "But you gave your baby and this one the hardest gift anyone can give when you traded them and took off to protect them. You can stop now, rest after just one more thing."

Hope washed her face and fled. She was afraid to hope. That made Jinx want to destroy everyone who'd stolen that hope from her with extreme prejudice. He breathed, careful not to disturb Dehmari.

Her lips compressed. She shook her head. "I don't know where he is. I let Fish take him. We had to…" She paused, swallowed. "We didn't know what else to do, so we shuffled them." A sad glance at the table. "I didn't think I wanted him. Didn't want that reminder. Who wants a demon's baby? And now, with her..." She turned to Bea. "With you... You gave us everything and we..." A glance at the knife Jinx had finally laid on the table. She put her face back in her arms. Her shoulders shook as she cried.

Tentatively, Bea reached over and touched her shoulder. Slid nearer and wrapped both arms around the teen. "Shh," she whispered. "It'll be okay. Whatever happens, it'll be okay."

Jinx regarded the two of them. He didn't want to make this harder than it had to be, but the kid in his arms had already thrown some serious temper tantrums in the short time he'd been here. There were few choices available.

"You can come back to San Francisco with me or stay here—" his gaze drifted to Bea, turned back to Magpie "—or go home. I don't know what it was like there for you or why you left, but this baby—" he shifted Dehmari to a more comfortable position in his arms "—cannot stay with you. She has to come with me, grow up learning how to be super human without killing anyone."

"I know."

It was said so softly that Jinx almost couldn't hear it.

Magpie sat up, and wiped her eyes and nose on her sleeve. Turned to Bea. "I don't know what I should do."

"You came all the way here from San Francisco," Bea said. "Where were you headed when I found you?"

Magpie sniffed. "Home." Panic crossed her face as she said the word. "But I don't think they want me. I don't know if—"

If they can accept who I am now and what I've done.

Jinx heard what she didn't say, the same way he could hear Luc. Telepathically. He tipped his head and gave her an odd look. Decided to give it a shot. *If they love you, they will,* he thought at her. *Do they?*

Instantly, Magpie startled and spooked, shoving herself away from the table and backing up to the kitchen doorway in a blink. "What are you doing? Don't. Don't ever!"

That answered that question.

It also solidified something he'd suspected, but hadn't been able to prove—why

Magpie, and girls like her, had been targeted by Michael Beck.

Because every single one of them had untapped special abilities.

17

"You're a telepath," Jinx said.

Fear flooded through Magpie. No one was supposed to know that. She'd run away from home because of it. Because her family hadn't known what to do with her, because their church refused to accept her, because her siblings were afraid of her and what she might tell their parents about them—tattle on them.

And she had done, when she was small, and their thoughts were loud in her head.

The same way, she was realizing, some of Jinx Falken's thoughts were now loud in her head.

Things like *Is this why you're not sure about going home?*

And like *I know someone who can help you figure this out.*

And *You can always come back to San Francisco with me.*

And *You are not a freak. Let me help you.*

She knew she wasn't imagining it because he nodded and said, "It's all right."

Because somehow, she knew he'd done something to open her mind and connect them telepathically.

Unnerved and frightened, she hugged the door frame and stared at him.

"Not me," he assured her. "I only issued the invitation."

"Don't," Magpie whispered. "It's wrong. I can't... I don't want..."

Jinx didn't take his eyes off of her. "You can *not* want this all you like, but you have a gift."

"What?" Bea asked. "What's happening?" Turned an accusing glare on Jinx. "What did you do?"

Jinx shrugged. "Showed her a door and invited her to walk through."

Bea stared at him. "You what now?" When he didn't respond, she turned to Magpie. "Tell me. Maybe I can help.

Magpie shuddered and shook her head. This wasn't anything anyone had ever been able to help with. She'd dealt with this curse all her life—until she'd been raped and gotten pregnant. Then the curse had been gone and she hadn't been bothered by it for over sixteen months.

The only positive thing to come from that encounter with Michael Beck.

And now the curse was back. She cast a resentful glance at Jinx. Because of *him*.

"You needed to know," he said quietly, and shifted Dehmari to a more comfortable position. The baby heaved a snuffly, heartbroken breath and quieted. "Because of her. Because of your own baby. You needed to know why."

Magpie shut her eyes. "He's not the only one, is he? Who'll try to find me and the others because of…" her face twisted with self-loathing "…*that.*"

"Because you're a telepath with the ability to mind read if you apply yourself, yes."

Magpie heard Bea gasp. "You can read minds?"

Magpie flinched at the accusation, looked wildly around, avoiding her rescuer's gaze. "I...no. Maybe. Sometimes. I used to. Not well. Not lately. Not here. Not you." Emphatically. "I *haven't*." Her gaze settled briefly on Bea then fled. She heard herself beg, "We like it here. Everything's so *shiny*. Please don't throw us out."

Bea's mouth opened, closed. She regarded Magpie, nonplused. She turned to Jinx. "Tell me. Right. Now. What is going on?"

"I'm the leader of the Brotherhood of Shadows," Jinx said bluntly. "I'm here to find and protect Magpie and Dehmari from some people who want to use them or kill them or use them then kill them because they represent the next stage of human development and they were born at least a century before they should be."

18

Silence followed this pronouncement. Judging by the looks Bea and Magpie were giving him, he was going to regret that reveal, Jinx knew it. He sighed. He didn't know why he said it, but had a feeling that somewhere in the aether, Aurora Montgomery was laughing at him.

In his arms, Dehmari fussed. He stroked her back, soothing. She kicked him. He swallowed a grin. She was going to be something contrary for sure. If he gave her to Solaya—

"Why is it everything that comes out of your mouth sounds like gibberish?" Bea asked.

Jinx snorted and started to laugh. He liked this woman more by the minute. "It's a lot to take in," he agreed, when he got his laughter under control. "But I assure you, it's true."

"The man who raped me said something like that," Magpie said quietly. "But I think he wanted to…" She hesitated as though what she was about to say didn't make sense to her. "He said something about the babies somehow helping to make him immortal." She looked at Jinx. "And I don't think he just meant as in they'd be his descendants. I think he meant it literally. He said we were connected to him through them, that he'd be able to find us again, no matter where we were. That he'd make sure we had more babies for him—that he would feed our souls to his ancestors and create an army of our descendants." Once again fear paled her features. "You're sure he's dead?"

"Yes. I saw him die. He's not coming back."

"And that other man?" Her fingers fluttered in a vague gesture toward the rear of the house. "He can't..." She swallowed. "He can't hurt us either?"

"He might try," Jinx said honestly, "but the Brotherhood will take him and lock him away where he can't hurt anyone."

She bit her lip, clearly weighing her options.

"For what it's worth," Jinx told her gently, "you're still underage, so you should probably see your family at least long enough to show them you're safe and not alone."

Worrying her bottom lip, Magpie cast a glance toward Bea, toward Dehmari, down at her hands. "I don't... I'm... It's been over four years. I'm not the same as I was before I left."

"That's true," Jinx said. "But I'll bet they're not the same people you ran away from either."

Her face lifted, expression torn between hope and despair. "You think?"

He nodded. "They've had four years to worry about you, wonder if you're safe, if you're alive, what they did to make you decide to leave. Even if you don't stay, they need to know that you're alive."

"Christmas," Bea said succinctly.

Magpie looked at her.

"You said your family lives north of here. You can call them or we can call the police—"

"No." Magpie's voice rose in panic. "No police. I don't want—"

Bea held up a hand to stop her. "There will be a missing child report—"

"Actually," Jinx said, "the Brotherhood will deal with the police. I can even let your family know that you've been found and are safe, but they're still *your* family. They should hear it from you, even if you don't tell them anything except Merry Christmas."

When Magpie continued to hesitate, Bea said firmly, "You can stay here until the roads clear, then I'll drive you up. But you can't stay here, work here, unless you talk to your family first." She gestured at Dehmari, focused hard on Magpie. "And she can't stay at all, especially if she's not yours, and not with her—" a glance at Jinx, then at the knives he'd plucked from the air and placed on the table "—extremely specialized needs."

"I was just supposed to keep her safe." Magpie's voice was low. "Hide. Make sure *he* couldn't take her and use her. Or me." She, too, looked at the knives. "But she needs more than I can give her."

Jinx nodded. Dehmari needed someone who could do more than feed, clothe, and shelter her. She needed someone who could deal with her increasingly supernatural deeds as well as her more human requirements. Teach her how to use those abilities properly or not at all. And Magpie-the-telepath, too.

"I promise to take good care of her," he said. "I... have a place, a shelter and a home, for people like you and Dehmari. There're people you can trust, like the woman Fish trusted to help find somewhere safe for you to give birth. Like the women who were there when your baby was born. Like the man who helped to destroy the man who raped you, the others that want to use you and the babies."

Magpie eyed him steadily. "But you want me to go home first."

Jinx shook his head. "I think you should try to go home first, yes." When her features turned mulish, he added quickly, "Or at least call and talk to them. Let them know you're well. Then…"

He took a breath. *Carpe Noctem*, the club he'd built, owned, and modernized at least a dozen times in the last century, had been destroyed during the earthquakes and Watcher uprising late last spring. He'd made the commitment before leaving San Francisco to renovate it one more time, turn it into a safe haven for homeless teens and families and those who needed sanctuary from the supernatural creatures that hunted them. But saying it here, now, to Magpie, made him realize how much he wanted it to work. How much he wanted to help people—families with kids like her, and especially like Dehmari who had abilities and who needed to learn what to do with them.

"Then," he repeated, looking at her wary, hopeful face. "Then."

19

San Francisco, California.

Two days before Christmas.

At Jinx's and Bea's insistence, Magpie had called the only phone number she had for her parents. When no one had answered, Jinx had sent someone to check out the small, northern town where she'd lived. No one had seen or heard from her family in months. The house she'd runaway from sat empty on a big, overgrown lot at the end of a neighborhood street, its windows covered, doors locked.

A little creative B&E by Jinx's operative offered up the information that Magpie's family had left home in a hurry, leaving wet clothing in both the washer and dryer, pots on the stove, the vacuum cleaner in the middle of the living room plugged in. Televisions were on in two of the bedrooms.

Magpie hadn't known what to think or how to feel when he gave her this news. She'd never considered her parents and siblings would be anywhere but where she'd left them. Maybe they would have stopped looking for her, stopped caring if she came back, stopped believing she was alive, but they would have been there, right where they were when she'd turned her back on them and her siblings and run.

It took another day for the roads to be cleared, then several more for Jinx's operatives to discover and confirm her family was missing. During that time, he'd slept in the camper part of his Snowcat outside the chocolate maker's house, keeping an eye on everything.

Dehmari seemed to pick up on Magpie's uncertain moods, throwing more and more supernatural temper tantrums, frightening Magpie, Bea, and the other women. Jinx had interceded, collecting Dehmari and keeping her either strapped to his chest or back in a baby carrier, or in the camper with him so he could limit the amount of mischief she caused. Amazingly, she didn't seem to mind the near-constant confinement. Magpie figured the baby was plotting against him, but no vengeful misdeeds occurred.

In the end, it was clear to Magpie that the infant's needs had seriously surpassed her ability to provide for them. She hadn't wanted to leave

Bea and the rest of the chocolate makers, but she'd also grown somewhat attached to Dehmari. And the lure of Jinx's promise to make sure she got the training she needed to control her own abilities became irresistible.

Trepidation overtook her again the moment their plane touched down at a private airfield outside San Francisco. Her bellyful of butterflies was equal parts fear and anticipation that her life would get better. She understood living without hope, living from hand to fist, existing in constant dread of Bad Things Happening. But Jinx's promises, and her desire to believe in them was completely foreign. By the time a big, black SUV deposited them outside Jinx's former club, she was a trembling wreck.

Someone from security ushered them out of the SUV and into the club. There were still signs of the destruction that had occurred the night Magpie's baby had been born, but renovations were well under way. Carrying Dehmari, Jinx led her through a maze of corridors to an open area where more people were gathered than Magpie ever remembered seeing in one place before—and she'd spent the better part of four years moving from one homeless encampment to another.

Nothing in the place seemed familiar to her. She had a vague memory of having been brought through a spectral door opened by Aurora Montgomery from the warehouse where Fish had hidden her. Wracked by contractions, she'd been carried directly into a penthouse apartment overlooking the cloudy, night-dark city.

Within hours of giving birth, Fish had taken her baby and led Magpie down through the bowels of the then-nightclub, straight to the park where Dehmari's mother lay dying and in labor in one of the homeless camps. There'd been a down-on-her luck cocaine addicted doctor in the camp who'd nevertheless worked hard with what she had on hand to keep the girl alive. After the girl died, the doctor performed a rude C-section to retrieve Dehmari from her womb. Then she'd cleaned up the baby and handed her to Fish, who gave her to Magpie.

Lost in memories she'd rather not have, Magpie started when they entered a huge communal dining hall. Her eyes widened at the sight of lofty fir trees bedecked in glittery

decorations and lights that looked like they were

growing right out of the floor around the

perimeter of the room. Wrapped and bagged

presents sat everywhere—atop tables and chairs,

and piled high around the trees. She didn't think

she'd ever seen so much *Christmas* in one place

before, not even in the years "before" when her

family still visited Santa in a local mall. She

wanted to wake Dehmari to show the baby all the

shiny, but thought better of it. There was no

telling what Dehmari might see and *reach* for,

and Magpie didn't want to start off on the wrong

foot in their new life. Still, she couldn't resist

reaching out to stroke a tree bauble or two as

they started around the room. A couple were so

pretty that she found her hand closing to lift

them off the trees—before she remembered where she was, who she was with, and why she shouldn't if she wanted to make a good impression.

And then Jinx plucked the very angel she liked the best off the tree they'd just passed, gave her a wink, and handed it to her. She felt her cheeks and throat grow hot with embarrassment, but she clutched the treasure tightly, surreptitiously glancing at it as they continued their circuit of the dining hall.

A tall woman dressed in supple red leathers who seemed vaguely familiar met them when they were about halfway around the room. Jinx's face lit up and he stepped to the side to exchange a few words with her that Magpie couldn't hear. When the woman scowled at him, he grinned, said something else, and handed her the sleeping Dehmari. She accepted the baby as gingerly as one might a particularly cranky bomb. Then, holding the baby well out in front of her body, she sent Jinx a killing look, turned and walked briskly out of the room.

"She says she doesn't like babies, but there's no one who will take better care of Dehmari," Jinx said, when Magpie gave him a questioning look. "Come on. I'm told there are some people here you should meet."

He led Magpie across the room toward a cluster of tables where several spooked-looking and unnaturally quiet family groups appeared to be sharing a meal. Several of the adults looked familiar. Magpie thought maybe she'd seen them when she'd been on the street or in the camps. A wary looking man and woman flanked by one girl in her early teens, a pair of preteen girls, and a toddler who couldn't have been more than three or four caught her attention. She looked harder at them. And started to shake.

A warm hand cupped her shoulder and Jinx stooped to talk into her ear. "Your mother was just pregnant when you left," he said. "They didn't even know it themselves until you'd been gone for a couple of months. They spent three years trying to find you before they gave up. Then a few months ago the little one started floating stuff. Telekinetic, but not as powerful as Dehmari. Your other sisters started to display superhuman abilities about the same time. Your parents freaked. They didn't know what to do until someone in the telepathic matrix Aurora

Montgomery uses heard your sisters call for help around Thanksgiving when someone tried to kidnap the older girls. One of our people got to them in time and convinced your parents to bring them here."

"That's my family?" Magpie's voice was squeaky. "It can't be. I don't understand. They would never—"

"Go against their church teaching them that superhuman abilities are the work of the devil?" Jinx asked.

Numb, Magpie nodded. "They'd be punished if the church elders ever caught them. I was..." She closed her eyes and let the thought trail off.

Jinx's mouth twisted. "They tried to beat your gifts out of you."

Magpie wrapped her arms around herself, protecting herself from the memory. "I don't understand," she repeated softly. "I never thought they would change."

"They didn't want to," Jinx said grimly. "It was a hard choice. But after you went missing, they had to look at things differently. Especially when your sisters' abilities started to manifest." He turned her to face him. His voice was kind. "You can walk away, cut them out of your life. No one will fault you."

She blinked. "I don't…"

"Or you can say hello and see what happens."

For a long moment, Magpie simply stared at him, feeling afraid. Then the preteen she'd been, the girl who'd rebelled, came to the fore.

She straightened her spine and squared her shoulders. Gave Jinx a trembling and crooked but rakish smile.

"What the hell, it's Christmas, right?"

Without further waffling, she headed over to her family's table.

***

San Francisco, California.

New Year's Eve, 11:47:56 p.m.

Face like a thundercloud, Solaya Lawton bounced the over-excited Dehmari on her hip. Two upper and two lower teeth showed when the baby opened her mouth on a delighted scream and *reached* for the sparkling streamers dropping from the ceiling.

"No," Solaya said firmly when Dehmari caught one and immediately started to put it in her mouth.

The infant glared at Solaya and bared her new teeth, leaning forward in an attempt to bite the sorceress. Solaya countered by holding her well away from any vulnerable bits of her person and bopping the miscreant on the nose.

"No," she repeated. "No biting."

At that, Dehmari began to struggle, *reaching* even harder for things to put in her mouth that she shouldn't. Solaya captured her hands, holding them so she couldn't. Dehmari shrieked.

From his vantage point near a Christmas tree a few feet away, Jinx watched the battle and swallowed a grin. It had been like this ever since he'd handed Dehmari off to her when he, Magpie, and the baby had arrived two days before Christmas. Solaya didn't want to be in charge of Dehmari, yet she refused to pass her along to anyone else. The skirmishes between the two ever since had been epic.

When Dehmari once again tried to bite her and Solaya switched her around so the baby's back was to her front, Jinx took pity on her. Plucking a candy cane shaped cookie off a plate as he passed, he strode across the room. Dehmari squealed happily at the sight of him, shrieking with glee and making grabby-hand gestures when he held the cookie where she could see it. Solaya frowned at him when he gave the cookie to Dehmari then lifted her out of Solaya's arms and stood her on the floor. The baby grabbed his finger and took a few faltering steps around his legs before clinging to one of them and sticking the cookie in her mouth. She bounced in place a few times and sat down. Jinx sat on the floor with her and made a V of his legs to act as a playpen on either side of her. Dehmari made happy "numming" sounds and patted one of his legs.

Solaya crossed her arms and stared down at them. "I hate you both," she said.

Jinx laughed. "You don't."

"I do," Solaya repeated, wagging a finger between him and the infant. "Both of you."

Jinx grinned. Solaya tried so hard to appear tough and uncaring, but he'd seen her soften over the last week. Seen the way she looked at Dehmari when no one else was around.

He held out a hand to her, wordlessly inviting her to join him on the carpet. She stared at him for a moment, looking like she wanted to. Then she thought better of it, folded her arms around herself, and continued to stand.

Jinx nodded to himself. His relationship with her was a work in progress. His hope for the coming year was that they would make some.

In the center of the dining hall, the grandfather clock began to *bong* the first of the twelve strokes that signaled the end of the old year and the start of the new. Jinx picked up the now sleepy Dehmari and got to his feet. Throughout the great room, people raised glasses of sparkling cider, toasting each other and the future.

Jinx looked around. Over to one side, Magpie sat with her family, still looking a little surprised by the dramatic turn her life had taken in the course of days. Her mother put an arm about her shoulders and gave her a hug. Her father slid an arm around them both while her siblings danced about yelling *Happy New Year* at the tops of their lungs.

Beside him, he felt Solaya lean in slightly, pressing into his arm as she leaned across to ruffle Dehmari's hair and rub her back before almost pulling away. Then he heard her sigh, felt her sag against him and wrap an arm through his, hugging.

Pure, unadulterated joy filled him. As gestures went, this one was huge. He risked stooping slightly to kiss the top of her head. She twisted to look up at him. Then she sighed, rose on tiptoe, and let her lips graze his cheek as the final stroke of midnight *bonged.*

"Happy New Year, Solaya," he mouthed.

And she, remarkably, said it back.

www.ingramcontent.com/pod-product-compliance
Lightning Source LLC
Chambersburg PA
CBHW021543150726
47990CB00006B/2383